3/21

DRAGON MASTERS

ROAR OF THE THUNDER DRAGON

BY
TRACEY WEST

ILLUSTRATED BY
DAMIEN JONES

BRANCHES
SCHOLASTIC INC.

DRAGON MASTERS

➤ Read All the Adventures ➤

More books coming soon!

TABLE OF CONTENTS

FOR BILL HANCOCK,

the King Roland to my Queen Rose. — TW

Text copyright © 2017 by Tracey West
Interior illustrations copyright © 2017 Scholastic Inc.

Library of Congress Cataloging-in-Publication Data
Names: West, Tracey, 1965- author. Jones, Damien, illustrator. West, Tracey, 1965- Dragon Masters; 8. Title: Roar of the Thunder Dragon / by Tracey West; illustrated by Damien Jones. Description: New York: Branches/Scholastic Inc., 2017. Series: Dragon Masters; 8 Summary: Lalo the baby Lightning Dragon has been taken by Eko, a rogue Dragon Master, who ran away with her Thunder Dragon years before—now she is back looking to gain control over all of the dragons in Bracken. Identifiers: LCCN 2016059062 ISBN 9781338042924 (pbk.) ISBN 9781338042931 (hardcover)
Subjects: LCSH: Dragons—Juvenile fiction. Wizards—Juvenile fiction. Magic—Juvenile fiction. Adventure stories. CYAC: Dragons—Fiction. Wizards—Fiction. Magic—Fiction. Adventure and adventurers—Fiction. GSAFD: Adventure fiction. LCGFT: Action and adventure fiction. Classification: LCC PZ7.W51937 Ro 2017 DDC 813.54 [Fic]—dc23 LC record available at https://lccn.loc.gov/2016059062

6 2020

Printed in the U.S.A.   23
First edition, September 2017
Illustrated by Damien Jones
Edited by Katie Carella
Book design by Jessica Meltzer

LOOKING FOR LALO

alo! Lalo!" Drake and Carlos called out as they walked through the trees. In front of the two Dragon Masters, a large brown dragon slithered along the path. Behind them, a short, chubby wizard named Diego watched the sky.

Together, they were searching for Carlos's dragon, Lalo. Carlos had only just met his Lightning Dragon when something terrible had happened. A woman named Eko flew into Carlos's land two days ago, riding a Thunder Dragon. She kidnapped Lalo!

Drake's Earth Dragon, Worm, had brought them to an island to look for Eko. Drake looked up at the trees. They were different from the ones at home in the Kingdom of Bracken. These trees had long, skinny trunks. Their green, ruffled leaves reminded him of feathers.

"Do you think we'll find her here?" Drake asked Diego.

"Maybe," the wizard replied. "Griffith's gazing ball showed Eko on an island a lot like this one."

Griffith, another wise wizard, was Diego's friend — and Drake's teacher.

Kee-kee! Drake heard a cry. He looked up to see a brightly colored bird fly across the blue sky.

3

"This would be a nice place to hide out," Drake said. "But I still don't understand why Eko kidnapped Lalo. She's a Dragon Master, just like me!"

Diego frowned. "As you know, Griffith teaches young Dragon Masters how to work with their dragons. Eko was his first student. She and Griffith often argued," he replied.

"About what?" Drake asked.

"Eko did not want to follow Griffith's rules," Diego replied. "And one day, many years ago, she left Bracken. She took her Thunder Dragon, Neru, with her."

"Did you go after her?" Drake asked.

"Yes," Diego replied. "But Griffith and I could not find Eko or her dragon. We have not seen them since — until two days ago."

Carlos had been quiet for a while. Now the dark-haired boy turned to Diego.

"Do you think we will find Eko and Neru now?" he asked.

Diego nodded. "There are more of us looking for them this time," he said.

Other Dragon Masters were out searching.
Bo and his Water Dragon, Shu. Ana and her
Sun Dragon, Kepri. Rori and her Fire Dragon,
Vulcan. And Petra and her Poison Dragon,
Zera. Griffith was in Bracken, watching over
them with his gazing ball.

"I just hope that Lalo
is safe," Carlos said.

Drake walked up
to Worm. His dragon
had tiny wings, but
he couldn't fly. He
didn't need to. Worm
could use the powers
of his mind to travel
anywhere.

"Worm, I know you can sometimes use
your mind powers to hear other dragons,"
Drake said. "Do you hear Lalo?"

Worm shook his head — then his eyes
suddenly flashed green.

"What is it?" Drake asked.

Every Dragon Master wore a piece of the Dragon Stone that connected them to their dragons. Now Drake's Dragon Stone glowed green.

Worm looked up.

The sky turned black. A strong wind whipped up. A jagged streak of lightning flashed.

"That could be Lalo's lightning!" Carlos cried.

Then *boom!* Thunder crashed. Lightning flashed again. This time, it hit the ground next to them, sizzling.

"This is a dangerous storm!" Diego yelled over the roaring wind. "We must go!"

He touched Worm. The boys did the same.

Before the next bolt of lightning flashed, they all disappeared.

KING ROLAND'S BIG NEWS

Drake's stomach flip-flopped as Worm transported them to Bracken. They landed inside the training room in King Roland's castle.

"Drake! Carlos! You're back!" Bo cried.

Drake blinked. His friends Bo and Ana were running toward him, followed by Griffith. The tall wizard looked happy to see them.

"You didn't find Lalo, either?" Bo asked.

Drake shook his head.

"We went to an island," Bo continued, "and we looked everywhere."

"So did we," Drake said. "But then a bad thunderstorm kicked up and we had to leave."

Griffith raised an eyebrow. "A storm?"

"A bad storm," Diego said. "Neru and Lalo might have caused it, but we couldn't stay to find out."

"When can we go back?" Carlos asked.

"Let's return to my cottage," Diego said. "We can use my gazing ball to see when the island is safe."

"Let us know what you find," Griffith said.

Diego waved his wand.

Poof! Diego and Carlos disappeared.

Just then, Rori and Petra came into the room. Red-haired Rori was frowning.

"Why did you make us come back?" Rori asked, looking at Griffith. "We were close to finding Lalo. I know it!"

"Actually, King Roland requested that you all return," Griffith replied.

"I'm glad we're all together," Petra said. "I'm not sure if Rori and I could fight Eko on our own."

"I'm not afraid of Eko," Rori said.

"You should be," Griffith said. "Over time, Eko has learned to tap into the powers of her dragon. This makes her very strong."

"Will we be able to tap into our dragons' powers, too?" Drake asked.

Griffith nodded. "Yes, but learning that takes many years. And I hope that you will all use that power to do good. Eko has chosen another path."

"All stand for King Roland!"

Two royal guards entered the room. Everyone got quiet. King Roland stomped down the stairs. His red cape flapped behind him.

"Wizard! Dragon Masters! I have news," King Roland said. "I am going to marry Queen Rose of Arkwood!"

Ana clapped her hands. Petra made a squealing sound. Drake and Bo exchanged happy looks. *Queen Rose is so kind*, Drake thought. Even Rori smiled.

"Congratulations, Your Highness," Griffith said. "When is the wedding?"

"Tomorrow!" King Roland replied. "There will be a big celebration, and I want it to begin with a parade of dragons."

"We will get to work on it right away, my king," Griffith promised.

"Very good!" the king said as he turned to leave. "I expect the most wonderful parade ever seen. Do not disappoint me!"

A LITTLE HELP FROM MAGIC

"We can't plan a silly parade!" Rori said. "We have to keep looking for Lalo!"

"Carlos and Diego are looking for Lalo," Griffith said. "We must obey our king."

Rori frowned but didn't argue.

"There is so much to do!" Petra said.

"This is so exciting!" Ana exclaimed. She ran into the classroom and everyone else followed her in.

Then she began to draw.

"King Roland and Queen Rose need to make a grand entrance!" she said. "They should ride through the village in a fancy carriage, pulled by dragons!"

"Shu would be honored to pull the carriage," Bo said.

Ana nodded. "Kepri too. They both can pull the carriage." She started drawing again.

"Our dragons should do tricks to show off their powers!" Rori said. "Vulcan could shoot fireballs!"

"Fireballs are dangerous," Griffith said. "Let's try to think of safe things your dragons can do."

Rori frowned and folded her arms.

"Zera could sing," Petra said. "She has a beautiful voice."

"Hmm. I'm not sure what Worm should do," Drake said.

"You'll think of something, Drake" Ana promised. She held up a drawing of a fancy carriage. "How's this?"

"It's perfect!" Bo said. "But where will we get a carriage like that by tomorrow?"

Ana looked at Griffith. "Could you use magic?"

Griffith stroked his beard. "I could do a transformation spell," he said. "But I need something to transform. Something round, and white..."

"An onion!" Drake cried. "I'll get one!"

Drake ran off and soon returned with a big white onion from the kitchens.

"I bet my family grew this one," he said. "We're the best onion growers in the kingdom."

They all returned to the Training Room. Griffith placed the onion and the drawing on the floor.

"Stand back!" he said.

Griffith pointed at the onion. Sparks flew from his finger. They hit the onion.

"A simple onion is what we see, but a kingly carriage you shall be!" he rhymed.

The onion began to grow and grow!

A big, white carriage sat where the onion had been. The carriage was made of wood carved with flowers. It looked just like Ana's drawing.

"It's perfect!" Ana cried.

"This is a wonderful start," Griffith said. "Come! We have more work to do before the wedding!"

CHAPTER 4

A PARADE OF DRAGONS

oday's a beautiful day for a wedding!" Ana cheered the next morning.

"There isn't a cloud in the sky!" agreed Bo.

The Dragon Masters were outside the castle doors, ready for the wedding parade to begin.

Each Dragon Master was wearing new clothes made by the king's tailor. Ana wore a yellow dress that shone like the sun. Bo wore a silky blue tunic with a wave stitched onto it. Rori's dress was as red as fire with a high, ruffled color. Petra's green dress had long sleeves and a short train behind it.

Drake looked down at his yellow shirt and brown pants. His new outfit was a lot like his old one, only neater and cleaner.

"I love how we match our dragons," Petra remarked. "You look like a Fire Dragon Princess, Rori!"

Rori smiled. "Thanks," she said. "But can I be a Fire Dragon Warrior instead?"

"Of course you can!" Petra replied.

Griffith appeared. "Places, everyone! The king and queen are coming!"

Rori ran to Vulcan, who was leading the parade. She climbed up and sat in a saddle. Puffs of gray smoke streamed from her Fire Dragon's nostrils.

Drake picked up two buckets filled with flowers and ran to Worm's side.

Worm stood next to Petra and her Poison Dragon, Zera. Each of the hydra's four heads was smiling.

Behind them, straps connected Kepri and Shu to the magical white carriage. Ana and Bo rode on their dragons.

Just then, King Roland and Queen Rose stepped on to the balcony.

The king wore his royal garments.

Queen Rose wore a long, white gown with red roses stitched all over it. Her eyes got wide when she saw the parade. "Roland, what a lovely surprise! You know how much I adore your dragons."

The king and queen came out of the castle. King Roland opened the door of the carriage.

"After you, my dear," he said.

Then they both climbed inside.

"Let the wedding parade begin!" King Roland announced.

The castle gates opened, and the dragons stepped forward, led by Griffith. Villagers from Bracken and Arkwood clapped as the parade made its way to the wedding grounds.

Vulcan flew into the air. Orange and red sparks shot from his nose. The crowd cheered.

On the ground, Zera began to sing. Sweet tones drifted over the crowd.

"Now, Worm," Drake said, and his dragon's eyes began to glow green.

Flowers floated out of Drake's buckets! They bounced and danced in the air like butterflies. Kids jumped up to catch them, giggling.

The loudest cheer went up as Kepri and Shu pulled the white carriage through the crowd. King Roland and Queen Rose waved to the villagers.

"Huzzah for King Roland! Huzzah for Queen Rose!" everyone cheered.

Suddenly, without warning, the sky grew dark. A wind whipped up. Lightning flashed.

"Take cover!" Griffith yelled.

The villagers rushed to stand under one of the wedding tents. King Roland pulled Queen Rose away from the carriage window.

A loud roar filled the air — a roar like thunder. *Booooooooooom!*

Drake looked up.

A hole made of purple, swirling energy appeared in the sky. Eko and her dragon swooped down from the hole! A baby Lightning Dragon flew behind them.

"Lalo!" Drake yelled.

EKO'S DEMAND

want the dragons!" Eko called out. "Release them to me and I will leave."

Drake and the other Dragon Masters stared up at Eko and her Thunder Dragon. Eko had black hair and piercing eyes. A glowing green Dragon Stone hung around her neck.

Dark purple scales rippled down the long body of the Thunder Dragon. Its four legs had big claws. Whiskers flowed from its snout.

The Lightning Dragon hovered behind the Thunder Dragon.

Drake saw a dark whip of purple light connecting Lalo to Eko. *Lalo can't get away,* he thought. *Eko is using Neru's powers to control him!*

"Give me the dragons!" Eko repeated, and her voice carried across the courtyard.

"Eko, give Lalo to us!" Griffith called up to her.

"Never!" Eko replied. "And I will not leave without the other dragons."

King Roland shook his fist at her. "These dragons belong to me!"

Eko glared down at the king. "Dragons belong to no one!" she cried.

"Then let Lalo go!" Griffith yelled. "You don't care about him. You're only using him to cause this storm."

"This Lightning Dragon should be with my Thunder Dragon!" Eko yelled. "They belong together!"

Booooooooooom!

Neru roared loudly. Drake felt the earth shake under his feet! Lalo flapped his wings nervously, shooting out sizzling sparks. The terrified villagers screamed and ran away.

Drake glanced at the other Dragon Masters. They looked stunned and scared. *But where are Rori and Vulcan?* he wondered.

Griffith stepped forward. "Eko, enough! We'll let you fly away if you stop this now!" he called up to her.

Eko laughed. "You'll *let me* fly away? I'm

the one in control now, Griffith. Neru and I are more powerful than ever!"

Booooooooooooom!

The Thunder Dragon roared again. Drake had to cover his ears.

Then Drake saw something red streaking across the sky. Rori swooped down, riding Vulcan! Her eyes looked angry as Vulcan dove toward Eko and the Thunder Dragon.

"Blast them, Vulcan!" Rori yelled.

BATTLE IN THE SKY

Rori, no!" Griffith yelled.

But Vulcan had already launched a fireball at the Thunder Dragon. As it hurled through the air, Neru roared again.

Booooooooooom!

This time, purple energy lines appeared, surrounding Neru and Eko. The big fireball bounced off the purple lines and landed in the grass. The grass burst into flame!

Bo climbed back up on Shu. He unleashed her from the carriage. "Shu, water blast!" he commanded.

Shu quickly shot water on the fire, putting it out.

Up in the sky, Eko turned to face Rori.

"Foolish girl!" she cried. "Your dragon is no match for mine!"

Rori ignored her. "Vulcan, fire!"

"Rori — no!" Griffith yelled. "Stop! It's too dangerous!"

Vulcan launched another fireball. Once again, Neru roared, and the flame bounced off the purple energy shield. It whizzed right over Drake's head and landed in the grass next to the carriage.

Shu put out the flames.

"I must contact Diego!" Griffith said as he took a small gazing ball from his pocket. "I will need his help to create a magic bubble strong enough to hold Eko and Neru. Rori won't listen, so I need all of you to protect your dragons and also the king and queen!"

Ana spoke to Kepri. The Sun Dragon raced forward, pulling the carriage back toward the castle.

At the same time, Vulcan shot another fireball. It hit the purple whip connecting Lalo to Eko.

Lalo broke free, raining sparks down on the carriage.

"Worm, get the king and queen to safety!" Drake yelled.

Worm's eyes glowed green. In a flash, he transported to the carriage. In another flash, Worm, the carriage, Ana, and Kepri disappeared.

Then Drake heard Worm's voice inside his head. *All safe inside the castle.*

Above, the frightened baby dragon was flying in circles and shooting sparks.

Then Drake heard a sound. He turned to see Zera singing. The song was sweet and calming. Curious, Lalo started to fly toward the hydra.

But then . . . *booooooooooom!* Neru's roar rocked the courtyard. Lalo shrieked and shot sparks. The boom hit Vulcan and knocked him out of the sky! Rori screamed as she and her dragon slammed into the ground.

"Rori!" Drake cried. He ran toward her.

"Nice try!" Eko called down to Rori. "Too bad you will never become a real warrior. Griffith will never teach you real power!"

"Stop this now, Eko!" Griffith yelled. He pointed at her, and a large, blue bubble began to form.

Eko laughed. "Your silly magic can't stop me, Griffith!" she cried. "These dragons are coming with me!"

FROZEN

Eko glared down at Griffith. "You will never capture us!"

Poof! Diego and Carlos appeared just in time.

"Diego, hurry! Add your magic to mine!" Griffith called out.

Diego looked up at the battle in the sky. He pointed, and blue light streamed out of his fingertips, joining Griffith's bubble. The two wizards pushed the magic bubble toward Eko and Neru.

At the same time, Carlos saw the baby Lightning Dragon.

"Lalo! I'm here!" he yelled.

Lalo's head turned at the sound of his name. He spotted Carlos. With a happy cry, he flew toward his Dragon Master.

"Lalo, no!" Eko yelled.

The wizards' magic bubble surrounded Eko and Neru.

"Good boy, Lalo," Carlos said as the baby dragon landed beside him.

"Neru, roar!" Eko commanded.

Boooooom! Neru roared, and the bubble wobbled.

"How about a freezing spell?" Diego asked, and Griffith nodded.

Then the two wizards chanted, "Frozen in space, frozen in time. Frozen in space, frozen in time . . ."

Inside the magic bubble, Eko and Neru stopped moving. The bubble gently floated down to the ground and faded away. Eko and Neru stood as still as statues.

Drake helped Rori up.

"Are you okay?" he asked.

Rori nodded. "Just some bumps, that's all."

Griffith marched up to her. "Rori, you must never use Vulcan to attack like that again!"

"I wasn't attacking, I was defending," Rori argued. "I stopped Eko from taking all of our dragons."

"What you did was very dangerous, Rori!" Griffith scolded. "You must learn to think before you act!"

"Somebody had to do something!" Rori shot back.

"You used your dragon's powers without my permission," Griffith said. "You cannot do that, Rori. You are still a young Dragon Master. You have much to learn."

Drake and Bo looked at each other. They were both thinking the same thing. *Rori is always arguing with Griffith . . .*

King Roland came out of the castle. He marched over to Griffith.

"What just happened here, wizard?" the king demanded.

WHAT NOW?

Griffith bowed to the king. "I am sorry," said the wizard. "We have captured the attacker." He pointed to Eko.

King Roland blinked. "Is this the Dragon Master who ran away with my Thunder Dragon years ago?" he asked.

"Yes, it is," Griffith answered.

The king's face darkened. "I must decide what punishment fits her best," he said.

"If you will allow me, Your Highness," said Griffith, "I will bring Eko and her dragon to the dragon caves for now. The frozen spell will wear off soon. But I will make sure that she does not escape."

"Very well," said the king.

He stomped back inside the castle.

Griffith turned to Drake. "Please go with Worm and transport Eko and Neru to the dragon caves," he said. "We will meet you there."

"Are you sure they won't unfreeze?" Drake asked nervously.

"You will be safe," Griffith promised.

Drake nodded. He looked up at Worm.

Worm snaked his body around Eko and her dragon. Drake touched Worm. Green light flashed as they transported with the still-frozen Eko and Neru.

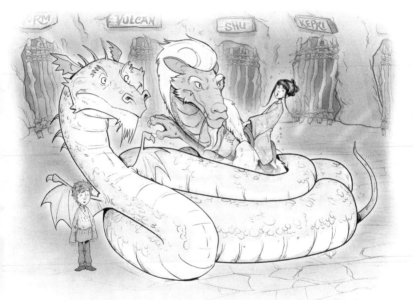

Even frozen, Eko's eyes glared with anger. Drake looked into them and shivered. He breathed a sigh of relief when the others arrived a few minutes later.

"Everyone, put your dragons inside their caves!" Griffith ordered. "Carlos, I have a cave ready for Lalo. I will put Neru in the cave beside him."

"Before," Drake began, "you said that Neru and Lalo have a special connection."

Griffith nodded. "Combined, their powers are very strong," he said. "I am sure that is why Eko stole Lalo."

Then the wizard pointed at Neru and surrounded him with a bubble of blue light. The bubble floated above the ground and into the cave.

"Neru will not harm us if Eko cannot control him," Griffith said.

"Now where should we put Eko?" Diego asked.

"I have a special cell in mind," Griffith replied. "Please remove her Dragon Stone and follow me."

"Right!" Diego answered.

Diego removed Eko's Dragon Stone and handed it to Griffith.

Then Diego captured Eko in a magic bubble.

Griffith went over to the wall. He placed his hand on a slab of stone and pushed on it. A door opened, revealing a tunnel.

"A secret tunnel!" Bo whispered to Drake.

"Everyone go to the classroom, please," Griffith instructed. "We will meet you there shortly."

Griffith nodded to Diego, who still held Eko in a magic bubble. The two wizards headed into the tunnel.

The Dragon Masters started to walk to the classroom. Petra looked back.

"Why does Eko want to steal all of our dragons?" she asked.

"I do not know," Drake answered. "She couldn't control our dragons if she got them. They only listen to us, their Dragon Masters."

"But she used Neru's powers to keep Lalo prisoner," Carlos said. "Could she do that to our dragons, too?"

"Maybe she could," Bo said. "But that would take a lot of power."

They entered the classroom.

"What do we do now?" Petra asked.

"We wait, I guess," Drake replied.

Bo, Ana, Carlos, and Petra sat down and kept talking. Rori paused by the door. Drake kept his eye on her. He watched as she left the room.

What's she up to now? Drake wondered. *I hope she's not getting into more trouble!*

Drake glanced at the other Dragon Masters. They were still talking about Eko.

He quietly slipped out of the room.

EKO'S STORY

Drake saw Rori just up ahead. She was hurrying down the tunnel leading to the dragon caves.

Is she going to visit Vulcan? Drake wondered. He kept following her. But she passed right by the dragons. She entered the secret tunnel leading to Griffith and Diego — and Eko.

When Drake caught up to Rori, she was standing outside Eko's cell. She frowned when she saw Drake. She put a finger to her lips.

"We shouldn't be down here. What are you doing?" Drake whispered.

Rori frowned. "Listen!" she hissed.

"Why, Eko, why?" Griffith was saying from inside the cell. "What do you want with our dragons?"

"They are not *your* dragons, Griffith!" Eko replied. "They never were. Just like poor Neru was never yours to take."

The wizards were silent.

"That's right, you can't deny it," Eko said. "I know that Neru was taken from his family."

"Eko," Griffith said. "It was for the best. You and Neru were meant to be together. The Dragon Stone chose you to connect with him."

"But Neru didn't choose to serve your greedy king," Eko replied. "That is why I had to free him."

Then Drake heard Diego's voice. "Eko, how is Neru free?" he asked. "He is with you, not his family."

"I gave him a choice, and he chose to stay with me," Eko said. "He had been away from his family for too long to go back. But it is not too late for the other dragons. I knew that if I was more powerful, then I could rescue more dragons from greedy rulers like King Roland. So I spent years learning how to use Neru's powers as my own. And then I heard about a lost baby dragon."

"I saw you use your powers to keep Lalo with you," Griffith pointed out. "He is not free."

"And Lalo was created by the prime Dragon Stone. He has no family except for Carlos," Diego added.

"He still has a right to be free if he wants, when he is old enough," Eko said. "The other dragons, they can be free now."

"I do not believe that you really want the dragons to be free," Griffith said. "I fear you want them for your own gain."

"You have never trusted me, Griffith," Eko said. "And you have not changed. I can tell you did not trust that fiery girl today — the only brave one among your new Dragon Masters."

Drake glanced at Rori. Her eyes were wide.

"You never gave me a reason to trust you," Griffith replied. "You could have talked to us about your concern for the dragons. Instead, you attacked. You'll never change."

"We should leave, Griffith," Diego said. "Eko is as stubborn as ever. She will not listen to us."

Rori tugged on Drake's sleeve. "Let's go!" she whispered.

Rori and Drake ran down the tunnel.

Drake's mind was racing faster than his feet. He kept thinking about one thing Eko had said — about Neru being taken from his family.

Worm had once showed Drake a vision. King Roland's soldiers stormed into a cave of Earth Dragons. They took Worm from his family. Worm had felt so afraid.

Is Eko right? he wondered. *Would Worm be better off without me?*

CHAPTER 10

WHO IS RIGHT?

Rori and Drake ran into the classroom. The other Dragon Masters rushed over.

"Where did you two go?" Ana asked.

Rori didn't answer. She turned to face Drake. Her eyes blazed with anger.

"Why did you follow me?" she asked.

"I just wanted to see where you were sneaking off to," Drake said. "In case you were up to something."

Rori folded her arms across her chest. "What does *that* mean?"

"It means Griffith was right: Sometimes you do act without thinking, Rori," Drake blurted out.

Now Rori's voice sounded hurt. "Is that what you really think, Drake? You're taking Griffith's side? *Really*?"

"Look at what happened today," Drake replied. "Eko attacked, and then you attacked Eko..."

"And Griffith told you to stop, but you didn't," Petra added.

"You, too, Petra?" Rori asked. "Eko was going to take our dragons! And now we know why."

Bo's eyes got wide. "Why? What did you hear?"

"Eko thinks King Roland was wrong to take the dragons from their homes," Rori said. "She thinks they should be free."

"But we are connected to our dragons," Bo said.

"They *want* to stay with us," Ana chimed in. "Remember when I asked Kepri if she wanted to stay in the Land of Pyramids? She chose to stay with me."

"And Zera has no home to go to," Petra said. "She loves it here!"

Rori frowned. "I guess. But I know Vulcan misses his family sometimes. He tells me so."

"It's confusing," Drake said. "I agree it was wrong for King Roland to capture the dragons the way that he did. But I think we were meant to be paired with them."

"Just think about all the good we've done together," Ana pointed out.

"And remember what Griffith said about the Dragon Stone," Drake said. "It brings dragons and their masters together for a reason."

"Maybe King Roland could stop using his soldiers to capture dragons," Ana suggested. "There must be a better way."

Drake nodded. "We could ask Griffith to talk to him, Rori."

Griffith and Diego stepped into the classroom.

"Rori, I am very unhappy with you for disobeying me today," Griffith said. "But I would like to thank the rest of you for following directions. You did well."

Rori scowled. "I did what I thought was right," she said. "I defended the castle from Maldred once, remember?"

"Yes, but today your actions put many people in danger," Griffith said. "You are still a student, and I am your teacher. You need to do what I say."

Rori balled her hands into fists. She looked down at the floor.

"What happens now, to Eko and her dragon?" Ana asked.

"I will deal with Eko," Griffith replied. "I can make her see that she is wrong. I will —"

"You will do nothing! I will deal with Eko!"

The Dragon Masters gasped as the king marched into the classroom.

KING ROLAND'S DEMAND

I have made a decision about Eko," King Roland said to Griffith. "You will use your wizard magic to send her far, far away. But we will keep her dragon. We will give it a new Dragon Master."

"Your Highness," Griffith said, "I know I can speak —"

King Roland held up his hand.

"Stop, Griffith," he said. "Years ago, when you let Eko get away with my dragon, I did not punish you. But now she is a danger to us. You will do as I ask."

Rori stepped forward. "You can't take Neru away from Eko! A dragon and Dragon Master have a bond!"

Griffith put a hand on Rori's shoulder. "Your Highness, I have taken Eko's Dragon Stone from her, so she cannot connect with her dragon," he said. "I will ask the Dragon Stone to find a new master for Neru."

"This isn't right!" Rori argued. She brushed away Griffith's hand.

"Get it done, wizard! You have until dawn to banish Eko," King Roland ordered. "And I want to see you and your Dragon Masters in my throne room in one hour. Queen Rose and I will be wed in a simple ceremony."

"We will be there," Griffith replied, and the king left.

Rori sat down. She stared at her boots. Drake could see tears glittering in her eyes.

"Griffith, where will you send Eko?" Bo asked.

"I don't know yet," Griffith replied, and his voice sounded sad.

"Do you really have to send her far away?" Petra asked. "Maybe the king —"

Griffith interrupted her. "I do not agree with the king," he said. "But I must obey him."

A STRONG CONNECTION

Diego clapped his hands together. "You all have a wedding to prepare for," he said. "And Carlos and I must take Lalo back home."

"Let us go to the dragon caves," Griffith said.

Moments later, they all gathered around as Diego opened the door to Lalo's cave.

"Lalo, we're going to go home now," Carlos said, patting the baby dragon's head. "You will sleep in the stable at Diego's cottage."

The Dragon Stone around Carlos's neck began to glow. Carlos smiled.

"Lalo does not know words yet, but he sends me his feelings," he told the Dragon Masters. "Right now, he is calm and happy."

Diego stepped inside the cave.

"It's settled then. The three of us will head home. Have fun at the wedding, everyone!" Diego said. Then he looked right at Griffith. "And good luck!"

Poof! Diego, Carlos, and Lalo disappeared.

Griffith turned to the Dragon Masters. "Now we must get ready for the wedding. Let's get you all cleaned up."

The Dragon Masters' fancy outfits were torn and stained. Griffith pointed at Bo. Sparks flew from his finger.

Bo's blue tunic looked like new again. Griffith used magic to spruce them all up, one by one.

Drake was too lost in his own thoughts to enjoy the fun magic. *Did Worm miss his home?* he wondered. *If he wanted to be free, could I let him go?*

"Dragon Masters, please shine your dragons' scales," Griffith said.

Drake entered Worm's cave. He gave Worm mushrooms — his dragon's favorite snack. He shined Worm's scales with a brush.

"Worm, if you could go back home, would you?" Drake asked.

Worm turned his head to look at Drake. He was silent for a moment. Then Drake heard Worm's voice in his head.

Drake is my home.

Drake hugged Worm around the neck. "You are my home, too, Worm."

Then Ana and Petra burst into the cave.

"It's time for the king's wedding!" Petra announced.

CHAPTER

13

RORI

King Roland stood in front of his throne in the castle's grand throne room. Behind him stood Father John, the royal priest.

The Dragon Masters and Griffith joined the small crowd gathered for the wedding. Drake saw the people closest to the king and queen: lords and ladies and family members.

The royal musicians struck up a tune.

80

Queen Rose walked to the front of the big room. Her wedding gown still looked beautiful. Two young women walked on either side of her. They looked like her, and Drake guessed they were her sisters.

Queen Rose stopped beside King Roland. He held out his hands, and she took them.

Father John coughed. He adjusted the spectacles on his nose. "King Roland the Bold, do you love this woman, Queen Rose the Just?" he asked.

"Yes!" King Roland exclaimed.

"And Queen Rose the Just, do you love this man, King Roland the Bold?" Father John asked.

"I do," Queen Rose replied, smiling.

"Excellent!" said Father John. "I now pronounce you husband and wife!"

The crowd cheered. The musicians played a lively song.

The Dragon Masters joined in the great feast.

"This is more food than I have ever seen!" Bo exclaimed.

"I know," Drake said, filling his plate. For a little while, he forgot about Eko and the Thunder Dragon.

When the party was over, all of the Dragon Masters went to their rooms. Drake fell asleep right away. He dreamed of feasting and dancing . . .

Rori.

Worm's voice echoed in his head.

Rori.

Drake woke up. He jumped out of bed. He ran to the room that Rori shared with Ana. Ana was asleep, but Rori wasn't in her bed. There was a note. Drake picked it up.

Dear Ana, Drake, Bo, and Petra,

I had to help Eko. Griffith and the King should not punish her for trying to help the dragons. And it is not fair to take Neru away from his Dragon Master. Neru should be with Eko.

You all took Griffith's side against me. But Eko thinks I'm brave. I heard her say so. Together, we will free dragons around the world.

I am not coming back, but don't worry about me. Vulcan told me he will stay with me and help me. We will take care of each other.

Rori

Drake's heart pounded.

"Rori is gone!" he yelled, hoping his cry would wake the others. He raced downstairs to the dragon caves.

Right away, he saw two cave doors open: Vulcan's and Neru's. Worm was standing in front of the open caves. A force field of purple light surrounded his body.

VULCAN

"Worm, are you all right?" Drake asked.

Worm's green eyes flashed. So did Drake's Dragon Stone. He saw pictures in his mind. Worm was showing him what had happened.

The pictures stopped. Drake gasped.

Griffith and the other Dragon Masters ran up to him.

"Rori helped Eko to escape!" he cried. "And they took Vulcan and Neru with them!"

GONE!

"Eko did something to Worm!" Drake said. "Griffith, can your magic help him?"

The wizard nodded. He shot blue sparks from his fingertips. The sparks hit the purple energy around Worm. The energy disappeared.

"Neru's powers froze Worm so he couldn't stop them from escaping," the wizard explained.

"Worm saw Rori and Eko coming out of the secret tunnel," Drake said. "He showed me what happened. Rori had keys with her. And Eko was wearing her Dragon Stone."

"Rori must have taken Eko's Dragon Stone from my workshop," Griffith said.

Ana gasped. "I'm sure Eko forced her to do it!"

"I don't think so," Drake said. He showed Ana the note. "Rori didn't think it was fair to keep Eko and Neru apart. And she was mad at all of us for not sticking up for her after she and Vulcan attacked Eko."

"She should have talked to us!" Petra cried. "She didn't need to run away."

"I am worried about her," Drake said. "Rori thinks Eko is good. But I'm not sure if she can trust her."

"We need to go after them!" Bo said. "Rori could be in danger!"

"I am worried about Rori, too," Griffith said. "And we must find her before the king learns that two of his dragons have escaped."

"We don't have much time!" Drake said.

"I know Rori will listen to us when we find her," Ana said. "We're her friends!"

"We might have to battle Eko again," said Bo. "That won't be easy."

"We can do anything when we work together," added Petra.

"That's right," Drake said. "We can do this!"

Simon the guard marched into the dragon caves.

"Dragon Masters, you have a visitor!" he said.

"A visitor?" Griffith asked.

A girl walked up behind Simon. Drake could see a Dragon Stone hanging around her neck!

"My name is Mina," she said. "And I need your help!"

TRACEY WEST has always loved thunderstorms and thinks it would be cool to have a Thunder Dragon.

Tracey has written dozens of books for kids. She does her writing in the house she shares with her husband and three stepkids. She also has plenty of animal friends to keep her company. She has three dogs, seven chickens, and one cat, who sits on her desk when she writes! Thankfully, the cat does not weigh as much as a dragon.

DAMIEN JONES lives with his wife and son in Cornwall — the home of the legend of King Arthur. Cornwall even has its very own castle! On clear days you can see for miles from the top of the castle, making it the perfect lookout for dragons.

Damien has illustrated children's books. He has also animated films and television programs. He works in a studio surrounded by figures of mystical characters that keep an eye on him as he draws.

DRAGON MASTERS
ROAR OF THE THUNDER DRAGON

Questions and Activities

Who is Eko? Why are the Dragon Masters looking for her at the beginning of this book?

Why are Eko's powers stronger than the other Dragon Masters' powers? Reread pages 12 and 61.

Look at the picture on page 35. What do you think Lalo is thinking and feeling?

Why doesn't Griffith want Vulcan to use fireballs? Why is Griffith upset with Rori after the battle? Reread pages 37-38 and 70.

Do you think Rori made the right decision at the end? Why or why not? Write a paragraph explaining your opinion.